*It seems incredible but this book was written before my son
Eddie died and before the new baby was born two years later.
So I dedicate it to Elsie and lovely old Eddie. – M.R.*

To Leo and Molly – P.L.

First published in Great Britain in 2002 by
Frances Lincoln Limited, 4 Torriano Mews,
Torriano Avenue, London NW5 2RZ

British Library Cataloguing in Publication Data available on request

ISBN 0-7112-1488-3

1 3 5 7 9 8 6 4 2

Printed in Singapore

Lovely Old Roly

Michael Rosen
Illustrated by Priscilla Lamont

FRANCES LINCOLN

Poor Roly!

His legs are tired. His whiskers are sad.

He sleeps all day.

"I think he's going," said Dad.

We'll sit with you, Roly.

Poor Roly!
His fur is dry. His eyes are old.
"I think it's nearly time," said Mum.
We love you, Roly.

Poor Roly!
He died on the Tuesday.
We buried him in the evening.
Goodbye, lovely old Roly!

"Has he really gone now?" we said.
"Yes, but you won't ever forget him,"
said Dad.
"He'll always be in and around you
somewhere," said Mum.
Old Roly.

So we tried to play
What's the Time, Mr Wolf?
We tried to play Pogo Sticks.
And we even tried to play
Danger Dog.
But Roly was too near.

Mum said things
had to be done.
Breakfasts and bedtimes
and shopping.
That sort of stuff.

Breakfasts
and bedtimes
and shopping.

"Can we have a kitten?" we said.
"Can we have a puppy?" we said.
"Can we have a rabbit?" we said.

And it was no, not yet,
it's too soon.
Poor us!

So we played
What's the Time, Mr Wolf?,
and Pogo Sticks,
and Danger Dog.

Then, one day...
"Mum, there's a cat at the door!"
"I think she's hungry."
"Can we feed her?"
"She wants to come in."

And it was maybe,
all right, a little –
but outside. Not inside.

"Mum, the cat's here again!"
"I think she's hungry."
"Can we feed her?"
"She wants to come in."
And it was maybe,
all right, a little –
but outside. Not inside.

But – too late!
She was in, sniffing and
sneaking all over the place.

"Come here, cat!"

"Over here, cat!"

"On me, cat!"

And cat came to stay.
We called her Sausage,
because she's a sausage on legs.
A roly-poly sausage.
And Sausage plays
What's the Time, Mr Wolf?,
and Pogo Sticks,
and Danger Dog.

"I wonder why Sausage
came here?" said Dad.
"She knew this was a house
with no cat," said Mum.
"She knew this was a house
that wanted a cat," we said.

And Sausage is with us a lot.

Loads and loads and loads.

Very nearly all the time.

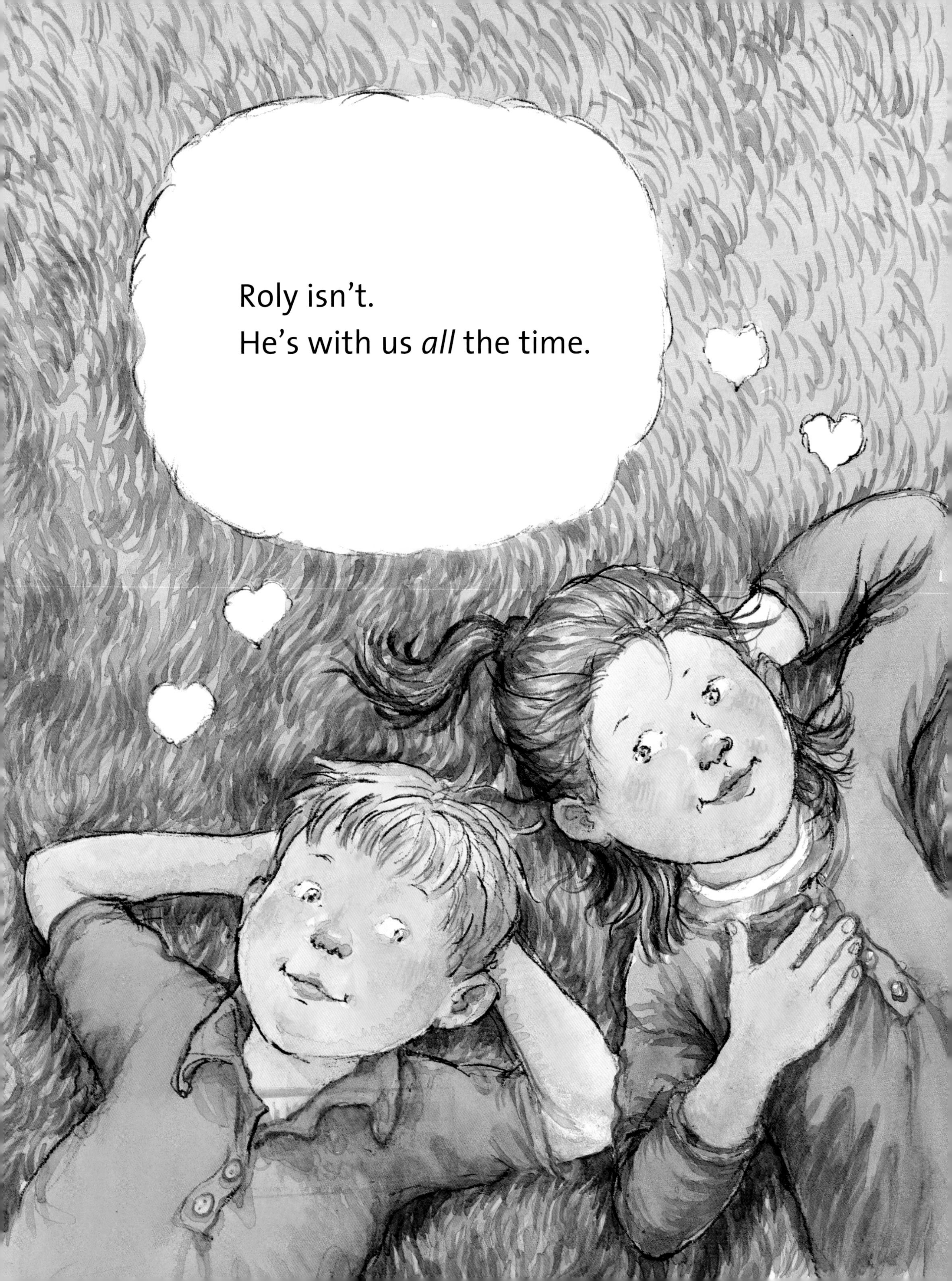

Roly isn't.
He's with us *all* the time.